D1345071

This book belongs to:

....

....

Written by Kath Smith
Illustrated by Caroline Jayne Church

This edition published by Parragon in 2009

Parragon
Queen Street House
4 Queen Street
Bath BA1 1HE, UK

ISBN 978-1-4075-6807-2
Printed in China

Wizards
are Magic

PaRRagon

Bath New York Singapore Hong Kong Cologne Delhi Melbourne

Scruffy Wizard Buffy

Buffy was a wizard who
was always good and kind.
So others always turned to him –
they knew he wouldn't mind.

If someone needed magic,
or something warm to wear,
they went to see their kindly friend.
He always seemed to care.

But though he was kind-hearted,
and *NEVER* cross or huffy,
Buffy had a little fault –
he always looked so scruffy!

His cloak was old and holey ...
a beggar had his best.
He never wore his wizard's hat –
it was a spider's nest!

As for Buffy's broomstick –
it was a mouse retreat.
So while the other wizards flew,
poor Buffy used his feet.

But Buffy never moaned at all.
He'd always smile and say,
"Take it with my blessing ..."
then he'd give his things away.

One day Fairy Lily came
to collect a special spell.
"He looks so tatty," Lily thought,
"he needs OUR help as well."

Off she flew to see her friends,
"He's such a dreadful sight!
His clothes are in such tatters.
It really is not right!"

When the others looked at him,
they realized it was true.
"Let's put our heads together,
to see what we can do!"

The princesses gave some jewellery –
the finest they could find.
The fairies gave some sparkle dust –
the magic, glowing kind.

The knights gave richest fabric –
nothing but the best!
The wizards cast a secret spell,
and magic did the rest.

They conjured up a splendid cloak,
a gift for kind old Buffy.
Delighted, Buffy laughed and cried,
"Goodbye to Mr Scruffy!"

Whizzy Wizard Izzy

Izzy, the whizzy wizard,
loved to race around.
Often he would move so fast,
he'd barely touch the ground.

Before he finished one thing,
he'd move on to the next,
I'm sure you can imagine,
this left some people vexed!

In fact, he was so speedy,
the other wizards said,
the only time he ever stopped
was when he went to bed.

Because he was so frantic,
his spells would rarely work.
When he twirled his wand around,
things often went beserk.

A magic sleeping potion,
could turn to mushroom stew.
And when he asked his broom to fly,
it knew not what to do!

Whenever someone came to lunch
and asked for tea or coffee,
they'd end up drinking something else,
like mud or sticky toffee!

He even turned poor Heather
into a tiny elf.
He went about his business –
SHE wasn't quite herself!

Then Heather said quite crossly,
"This time I've had enough.
Something really must be done
to stop this silly stuff."

So Heather, who was clever,
thought hard and gave a frown
then cried, "I've got the answer.
He must be slowed right down."

Izzy's problem was, you see,
he didn't stop to think.
But Heather put an end to that
with a bubbling magic drink.

Now when Izzy casts a spell,
he has to STOP and sneeze.
This gives him time to check it's right,
then cast his spell with ease.

Grumpy Wizard Dumpy

Far away in Wizard Wood
lived moaning Wizard Dumpy.
He never seemed to laugh or smile.
His face was always grumpy.

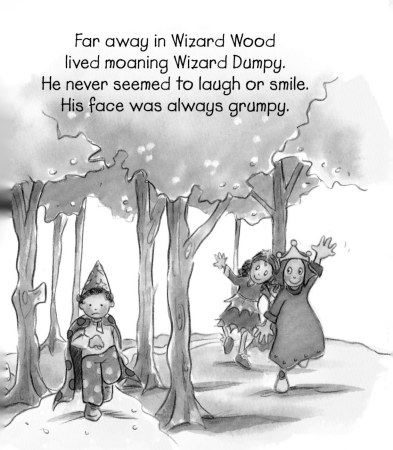

When someone said, "Good morning!"
he'd mutter, "What's so good?"
and when they shouted, "Hi, there!"
he'd ignore them if he could.

Dumpy was so surly,
he never joined in the fun.
He was, of all the wizards ther
the only grumpy one.

"A wizard shouldn't be so sad,"
decided Princess Polly.
"He needs someone to cheer him u
and make him far more jolly."

So Polly asked him riddles,
and told jokes that made her roar.
But Dumpy only sighed and said,
"What are you laughing for?"

Then early one fine morning,
she knocked on Dumpy's door.
But Dumpy did not answer,
and then she heard a snore.

She looked in through the window
as Dumpy left his bed.
Poor Dumpy didn't rise and shine,
but tumbled out instead.

As Dumpy's bed was floating,
the fall was rather bad.
If Dumpy fell like that each day,
no wonder he was sad!

Polly visited Fairy Heather,
who thought a bit, then said,
"I think something must be done,
to help him out of bed!"

So Heather waved her magic wand
in front of Dumpy's face.
Then, in a cloud of magic dust,
appeared a long staircase.

Now Dumpy starts his mornings
the way a wizard should,
by walking down a staircase ...
... and in a mood that's good!

29